Y0-BTX-548

A FOLLETT BEGINNING-TO-READ BOOK

Library of Congress Catalog Card Number: 59-8784

Nicholas P. Georgiady
and
Louis G. Romano

Gertie the Duck

Illustrated by Dagmar Wilson

Follett Publishing Company Chicago

Copyright © 1959 by Follett Publishing Company, a division of the Follett Corporation.
All rights reserved. No portion of this book may be reproduced in any form without
written permission from the publisher. Manufactured in the United States of America.

ISBN 0-695-43363-6   Titan Binding
ISBN 0-695-33363-1   Paper Edition

1415161718/828180797877

Gertie the duck was looking

for a place to build her nest.

She looked at a farm.

There were not many people there.

Gertie did not like the farm.

She looked at a lake.

There were only a few people
in boats on the lake.

Gertie did not like the lake.

Gertie looked at a swamp.

There were no people there.

She did not like the swamp.

Gertie the duck liked to be
near people.

She liked fat people, thin people,
tall people, short people.

She liked young people and
old people.

Gertie the duck liked people.

Where could she build her nest?

Gertie flew about looking

for a place.

She came to a big city.

She saw many people in the city.

But where could she build her nest?

On top of a tall building? No!

Could she build her nest on a sign?

No!

Gertie looked everywhere.

Where could she build her nest?

She saw a river.

Ducks like the water.

Gertie flew down to the river.

She saw a bridge.

There were many people
on the bridge.

In the water near the bridge
Gertie saw some large posts.

Gertie flew down to the posts.

The posts were old.

The wood was soft.

Gertie picked bits of soft wood
from the top of a large post.

Soon she had a good place
for a nest.

She sat in it.

It was just right.

Just above Gertie's nest was
the bridge.

Soon a little boy and his mother
went by.

The little boy saw Gertie.

"Look!" he said to his mother.

"See the duck down there!"

Other people stopped to look.

Fat people, thin people.

Tall people, short people.

Old people, young people.

Firemen, policemen. Bus drivers, truck drivers.

They all watched Gertie.

The men who worked on the bridge
watched Gertie too.

They watched from their little house.

Gertie was happy.

She had found a nest.

The nest was near water.

The nest was near many people.

And Gertie liked people.

One day Gertie flew away from the
nest to find food.

People saw three eggs in the nest.

They were very happy.

One day some men came to work on
the bridge.

They came to take out old posts.

The men saw Gertie in her nest.

They saw the eggs.

Now there were six eggs.

The men liked Gertie.

They did not take out the old posts.

Everyone watched Gertie.

Sailors watched her as boats went under the bridge.

People stopped their cars and watched Gertie.

She sat on her eggs to keep
them warm.

She sat on them for days and days.

The only time she went away was
to get some food.

She came back soon.

One day, out came a baby duck.

He was all black.

The people named him "Black Bill."

Soon the other ducklings came

out of the eggs too.

Black Bill did not like to stay
in the nest.

He liked to jump on his mother's
back.

He liked to walk on the posts.

He wanted people to see him.

Black Bill was a show-off.

One day Black Bill walked too far.

Splash! He fell into the water,

far below the nest.

The man who took care of

the bridge ran to help.

He took a long pole with a net
at the end.

He picked up Black Bill in the
net, and put him back in the nest.

But soon the other ducklings
began to fall in the water.

They could not get back in the
nest by themselves.

People were afraid they would
get lost.

Where could they put Gertie and
her ducklings so they would be safe?

At last the people found a
good place for Gertie and her family.

They moved the ducks to the park.

On moving day, everyone was there.

The mayor. The chief of police.

The fire chief.

The town band was there too.

Many other people were there.
They cheered as Gertie and her
family went by on a big red fire
engine.

There was a pond in the park.

Soon Gertie and her ducklings

were swimming about in the pond.

Every day people came to watch.

Gertie and her family were happy.

The people were happy.

The pond was a fine home

for Gertie, the duck who liked people.

GERTIE THE DUCK

Reading Level: Level One. *Gertie the Duck* has a total vocabulary of 177 words. It has been tested in first grade classes, where it was read with ease.

Uses of this Book: To develop kindness to animals and to give nature information. An interesting and entertaining story that children will enjoy reading. Useful as supplementary material in primary social studies.

Word List

All of the 177 words in *Gertie the Duck* are listed. Regular plurals *(-s)* and regular verb forms *(-s, -ed, -ing)* of words already on the list are not listed separately, but the endings are given in parenthesis after the word.

5	Gertie('s)		like(d)		about
	the	6	lake		came
	duck(s)		only		big
	was		few		city
	look(ing)(ed)		in		saw
	for		boats	9	but
	a		on		top
	place	7	swamp		of
	to		no		sign
	build(ing)		be	10	everywhere
	her		near		river
	nest		fat		water
	she		thin		down
	at		tall	11	bridge
	farm		short		some
	there		young		large
	were		and		post(s)
	not		old	12	wood
	many	8	where		soft
	people		could		picked
	did		flew		bits

	from		find		man
	soon		food		took
	had		three		care
	good		eggs		ran
	sat		very		help
	it	**17**	take	**23**	long
	just		out		pole
	right		now		with
13	above		six		net
	little	**18**	everyone		end
	boy		sailors		up
	his		as		put
	mother('s)		under	**24**	began
	went		cars		fall
	by	**19**	keep		themselves
	he		them		afraid
	said		warm		would
	see		time		lost
14	other		get		so
	stopped		back		safe
	firemen		quickly	**25**	last
	policemen	**20**	baby		family
	truck		black		moved
	drivers		named		moving
	bus		him		park
	they		Bill		mayor
	all		ducklings		chief
	watched		too		police
15	men	**21**	stay		fire
	who		jump		town
	work(ed)		walk(ed)		band
	their		wanted	**26**	cheered
	house		show-off		red
	happy	**22**	far		engine
	found		splash	**28**	pond
16	one		fell		swimming
	day(s)		into	**29**	every
	away		below		home

The Follett BEGINNING-TO-READ Books

Purpose of the Beginning-to-Read Books: To provide easy-to-read materials that will appeal to the interests of primary children. Careful attention is given to vocabulary load and sentence length, but the first criterion is interest to children.

Reading Levels: These books are written at three reading levels, indicated by one, two, or three dots beneath the *Beginning-to-Read* symbol on the back cover. *Level One* books can be read by first grade children in the last half of the school year. As children increase their reading ability they will be able to enjoy *Level Two* books. And as they grow further in their reading ability they will progress to *Level Three* books. Some first grade children will read *Level Two* and *Level Three* books. Many third graders, and even some fourth graders, will read and enjoy *Level One* and *Level Two* books, as well as *Level Three* books. The range of interest of *Beginning-to-Read* books stretches far beyond their reading level.

Use of the Beginning-to-Read Books: Because of their high interest and readability, these books are ideal for independent reading by primary children—at school, in the library, and at home. The books may also be incorporated into the basic reading program to develop children's interests, expand their vocabularies, and improve word-attack skills. It has been suggested that they might serve as the foundation for a skillfully directed reading program. Many *Beginning-to-Read* books correlate with the social studies, science, and other subject fields. All will help children grow in the language arts. Children will read the *Beginning-to-Read* books with confidence, with success, and with real enjoyment.